THE MINISTRY OF MISSIONS

THE MINISTRY OF MISSIONS

MISSIONS IS MINISTRY

Dr. Mark Rowden, ThD

Palmetto Publishing Group
Charleston, SC

The Ministry of Missions
Copyright © 2019 by Dr. Mark Rowden, ThD
All rights reserved

First Edition

Printed in the United States

ISBN-13: 978-1-64111-326-7
ISBN-10: 1-64111-326-X

"For I was hungry, and ye gave me meat: I was thirsty, and ye gave me drink: I was a stranger, and ye took me in: Naked, and ye clothed me: I was sick, and ye visited me: I was in prison, and ye came unto me" (Matthew 25:35-36 KJV).

CONTENTS

This book goes out with a special dedication to my loving wife, Beverly Rowden, with my heart filled with gratitude and appreciation for her unselfish support and genuine loyalty. Without question, she has been a true partner in ministry, and her continuous intercession for me, and the vision that God has given me, is a blessing.

INTRODUCTION

As I stood on the shores of West Africa, I was compelled to raise my hand and point out towards unknown territory, as if God was releasing me to *go*. It seems prophetic to me now, given the ministry that He has birthed through me. A ministry of, and for, missions. After receiving and responding to the call of God, he infused everything in me towards total servitude. It is a very humbling experience. I was now totally dependent on God to perform only what God could do, because I had no resources to fulfil this call.

Not knowing how he would do it, but very sure of what God was asking of me kept me in a prayer posture for this ministry of missions.

There I stood, alone out on this rock, solidly placed amid the motion of the waters, and I began to ponder the *how*. How could I give what I didn't have to a people who were truly in need? How would I find the resources to sow into the vision that God had birth in my spirit? I felt the joy of the Lord as he began to confirm in my spirit that he was with me, and that even though I stood on that rock alone, I would never be alone, because He would be with me. As the needs of the people revealed themselves while I was visiting West Africa, I would follow through immediately with a promise to deliver to the people the supplies that were needed. Now I had to truly trust God for His provisioning. When I thought of those who God would have me touch through prayer, or a spoken Word from God, or just a deed undone, my heart was overwhelmed, and I began to think about the compassion that Christ demonstrates in the earth.

At this point, I began to think about my desire to help God's people, and my mind traveled back to my childhood. Growing up on the streets of Houston, Texas, I remembered that at a young age, I always felt a need to help others. I started working at the age of twelve, doing a sales paper route. I was excited about my paper route, because I could make money other than the small allowance I was receiving from my parents for doing household chores and yard work. I could have money to help my friends who were less fortunate than me. My father, Troy Rowden, instilled in me and my siblings that if we wanted to have money, we needed to work for it.

My heart for outreach and helping others began as an elementary student attending Robert Lee Frost Elementary School in Houston, Texas. I did not know it then; however, whenever I saw another student sitting in the cafeteria not eating, I would ask them, "Why aren't you eating?" Sometimes they would simply say, "I'm not hungry," while other times, some would say, "I don't have a lunch, nor do I have any money to buy lunch." (Free and reduced lunches were not a huge part of the public school system back then.). So, I would either give them my lunch, or whatever money I had, so that they may buy a lunch.

Although it left me without a lunch, not having eaten, the joy I had inside of me meant more to me than the lunch. I would be so hungry waiting on dinner to be served once I was home, I would cry. Growing up in the sixties, the family would eat dinner together, and we had to wait until my father returned home from work before we could eat. Only God knows how hungry I was waiting on Daddy to get home. I recall one day my father came home from work, and I was crying because I was hungry. He asked me what was wrong with me, and I told him I was hungry but had to wait until he got home before we could eat. I remember it like it was yesterday.

I heard him tell my mother to never again make the children wait until he got home from work to feed us, because some days he may be late. I thought that was the day I was in heaven. Oh, what a relief those words were. My parents never knew that I was giving my lunch to someone less fortunate than me, but I truly believe God was planting a seed in me for the work of the ministry. This, I believe, was the beginning of having compassion beyond my understanding. And without fully understanding, this was the beginning of missions as ministry in my life.

My heavenly father has placed in me a burning desire to continue to provide for those less fortunate than me. Knowing that my station in life did not leave me with an abundance of wealth to fund this "Ministry of Missions," I am solely dependent on God, and the people of God who are likeminded, and those whose compassion is driven by the will of God.

LUKE 10:30-35 (NIV)

In reply, Jesus said, "A man was going down from Jerusalem to Jericho, when he was attacked by robbers. They stripped him of his clothes, beat him, and went away, leaving him half dead. A priest happened to be going down the same road, and when he saw the man, he passed by on the other side. So too, a Levite, when he came to the place and saw him, passed by on the other side. But a Samaritan, as he traveled, came where the man was; and when he saw him, he took pity on him. He went to him and bandaged his wounds, pouring on oil and wine. Then he put the man on his own donkey, brought him to an inn, and took care of him. The next day he took out two denarii and gave them to the innkeeper. 'Look after him,' he said, 'and when I return, I will reimburse you for any extra expense you may have'" (Luke 10:30-35 NIV).

My earnest prayer is that the body of Christ everywhere will move from Mission Meetings to Mission

Ministry. Missions must be considered, first and foremost, as a ministry. As a ministry, it must strive to meet the needs of others, rather than benefiting ourselves. Missions calls for sacrifice on part of the missionary. Missions should never be viewed as a time to vacation. If our aim is to be seen, or to please men, then all we are doing is going through the motions. God is not pleased when we just go through the motions.

WHAT IS MISSIONS?

Every church or ministry needs to have a well-thought-out philosophy of missions. Even churches and ministries that have given no thought to their missions strategy at all should have an effective philosophy of missions.

When Jesus issued the Great Commission in Matthew 28:19 KJV—"Go ye therefore, and teach all nations, baptizing them in the name of the Father, and of the Son, and of the Holy Ghost"—This did not limit us to missions in our local communities; in fact, He is clear that we must go into all the world (Mark 16:15). This is a global command.

When we explain one of man's greatest questions about the Great Commission, one must dissect the scriptural saying from Jesus. The "what" of missions, I have concluded, is as follows:

- Missions should be built into the heart, mind, body, and soul of the church. It has to be routine, and not exercised haphazardly as we go.
- The goal of missions is to reach all nations with the gospel.
- The goal of missions must focus on making disciples, not to take the place of governmental relief services.
- Baptism and teaching are functions of the local church; therefore missions, regardless of geographic location, ought to focus on the same.

Mark Rowden Ministry International, Inc. vision encompasses a holistic ministry of outreach. Our approach to missions is in a way that encourages the whole ministry to be personally invested in missions. This includes, but is not limited to, the board of directors, ambassadors and affiliates. MRM's goal is to approach missions in a way that focuses on the spiritual need of the lost, not on the physical needs of the poor.

We have taken an approach to missions in a way that is focused on strengthening local church ministries, as well as overseas churches and ministries.

We committed to approach missions in such a way as to have the greatest possible impact on teaching—reaching—restoring families, and creating a missional environment that epitomizes Matthew 29:18, with a limited, small ministry budget.

I have served as senior pastor for the Savannah Missionary Baptist Church, located in Fayetteville, North Carolina, for nearly two decades. In many missionary Baptist churches across the United States, missions has not been a priority; however, being mission-minded, I am grateful to serve as pastor of a missionary Baptist church that has heeded the clarion call in obedience to the mandate of missions from hurricane relief efforts that span from North Carolina to Texas, all the way to the Virgin Islands. We have met the many needs from food to clothing to ministering to the souls of those in need.

WHY MISSIONS?

PRIMARY PURPOSE OF MISSIONS

"Let your light so shine before men, that they may see your good works, and glorify your Father which is in heaven" (Matthew 5:16 KJV).

The need is compelling.

Humanity is lost, eternity is certain, and Jesus is the only way of salvation. If Jesus died for everyone, then everyone must be told.

Two thirds of the world's population has yet to receive an adequate witness of salvation in Jesus Christ. Allow me to explain.

Two-Thirds World *n.* [by partial analogy with *third world* "the developing nations of the world"] The geographical area comprising Africa, Asia, Latin America, and Oceania; this area as a locus of missionary work; this area as home to the majority of the world's

Christians, and to the majority of the world's population; the developing nations of the world (historically known as the Third World).

The term "two-thirds world" was coined in the late 1960s as an alternative to the term "third world," and it alludes to global population statistics compiled around that time that showed that this area of the world was home to approximately two-thirds of the world's population. The term started being used by some Christian missionaries and missiologists in the early 1980s.

In the 1990s, many commentators endorsed the term "two-thirds world," because the term was alleged to helpfully draw attention to the large number of Christians, and the large number of potential converts in this area of the world. The alternative term "third world," then in use, was alleged to be encumbered by out-of-date political overtones and derogatory connotations.

But starting in the 2000s, some commentators began to disapprove of "two-thirds world," alleging that it was unfamiliar and out-of-date.

I have traveled to several developing countries, and the natives will quickly correct you if you use the term "third-world country" to describe them. They would tell you they are a "developing country."

The command is clear.

The Great Commission is not optional for the church. Because of our Lord's command, every follower of Christ is responsible in some way to those who wait to hear the saving message of Jesus Christ. At some point or another, Christian leaders are confronted with the command of "Go". These are among the last recorded words of Jesus and therefore seem to carry a little more weight. Jesus was specific in what he wanted us to accomplish in our going "teach all nations, baptizing them in the name of the Father, Son and Holy Ghost" (Matthew 28:19).

The call demands a response.

For some of us, the question is this: Has God called me to go? What compels a person to leave the comforts and security of homes, family, and friends to serve Christ in a foreign land? The call.

Being a missionary is not a career choice based on human ambition. Saying yes to God's call means surrendering personal dreams and ambition on the altar of commitment.

For some, the call is dramatic and unforgettable. For others, it is a steadily growing realization that they have no alternative but to spend their lives taking the gospel to those who are waiting to hear. To those He calls, what matters most is not results, but simply obedience to the Master.

The disciples may not have realized it, but when Jesus gave them the Great Commission command in Matthew, Chapter 28, they were being commissioned "missionaries." Missiology is defined as the area of practical theology that investigates the mandate, message, and mission of the Christian church, especially the nature of missionary work. The call to follow Jesus comes with a call to missions. I believe every Christian (follower of Jesus) must practice missions in some form or another. Christian mission is an organized effort to spread Christianity to new converts, and to take the gospel abroad in order to have a global reach.

Why missions? Because there are more than four billion spiritually lost people waiting to hear the good news of salvation and eternal life. Jesus knows, and calls, each messenger personally. He knows each lost soul, and longs to reach each heart to let each one know of his love and salvation. This is evident when he says, "For the Son of man is come to seek and to save that which was lost" (Luke 19:10 KJV).

PRIMARY PURPOSE OF MISSIONS

"In the same way, let your light shine before others, that they may see your good deeds and glorify your Father in heaven" (Matthew 5:16 NIV).

I often say to other believers, "People don't really care how much we know until they know how much we care." In doing the Ministry of Missions, prayer and good conversation is encouraged; however, as it is declared in James 2:14, "Faith without works is dead."

In my experience on the mission field, I am of the opinion that a practical mission approach tends to reach more souls. Allow me to explain.

While working for the Cumberland County schools as the community liaison, I encountered many youth who lived in families like so many families around the world, who had their seasons of struggle, seasons of falling on hard times. As the community liaison, one of my main functions was to gather attendance data on chronically tardy students. Once the data had been collected, the truancy officer (Officer Kendra Faire) from the Fayetteville Police Department and I would visit the home to gather information from a parent or guardian in the home. On several visits to many of the homes, our knocks went unanswered. I would leave a business card with all of my contact information, as well as a card with Officer Faire's contact information, with a note on it that said "Please call." From some of the homes, no one would call either of us, even after several visits.

One day, I happened to run into one of the students whose name was on the chronically tardy list. I identified myself as a Cumberland County schools official, and what my position was. I then asked the student what their reason was for so many unexcused tardies. The student stated they did not own a winter coat; it was too cold outside to wait on the bus, and they would miss the bus. Immediately, my thoughts went back to the scripture, "Let your light shine before others, that they may see your good deeds and glorify your Father in heaven" (Matthew 5:16 NIV).

In order to fulfil the scripture, and live up to my own saying—that people don't care how much we know, until they know how much we care—I purchased a winter coat for the student, and gave it to the family. A positive seed was planted in the mind of this young student that I pray God will give the increase. A similar need was identified while visiting another family of a chronically tardy elementary school kid, whose parents stated they did not own an alarm clock, nor could they afford a cellular phone that would help to get them up on time each day. In my mind I was thinking, now here is a family with a young kid missing out on valuable instructional class time, just because they cannot afford an alarm clock. I asked the truancy officer to drive me to the local store, and I purchased an inexpensive alarm clock, took it back to the home, and gave it to the family.

These are just a couple of ministry opportunities of so many more that allow for the scripture to be fulfilled, and to demonstrate the love of Christ that is in us. When we let our light (the light of Jesus Christ) so shine, others will see our good deeds, and glorify our Father in heaven. The motive to influence us cannot simply be that we may be seen, but it must be that our heavenly Father may be glorified. The Pharisees acted to be seen of men; true Christians act to glorify God, and care little what people may think of them, except as by their conduct others may be brought to honor God, yet they should so live that people may see from their conduct what the proper nature of their religion is. (Matthew 5:14-16).

Jesus demonstrated, time and time again throughout scripture, the love of God, and His compassion for people in order that God the Father would be glorified.

When God is glorified—that is, when the ministration of the Gospel has been blessed for the illumination of the minds of men, to a thorough conviction of their state, and for their regeneration, conversion, sanctification, and comfort—they may give praise to God.

THE MOTIVATION FOR MISSIONS

COMPASSION

"When Jesus landed and saw a large crowd, he had compassion on them, and healed their sick" (Matthew 14:14 KJV).

Missions must be motivated by *mercy* and *compassion*. Matthew 9:27 teaches, "[A]nd when Jesus departed thence, two blind men followed him, crying, and saying, 'Thou son of David, have mercy on us.'" Matthew 14:14 reveals, "And Jesus went forth, and saw a great multitude, and was moved with compassion toward them, and he healed their sick." A true missionary must be one with compassion for the needs of others unselfishly; meaning, there are those who will see their own personal needs, and allow it to overshadow the true needs of others.

I was in a local cleaners turning in some clothes to be laundered for an upcoming missions trip to West

Africa. There was a lady inside who said to me, "She wants to ask you something," speaking of one of the other employees who'd overheard me talking about the upcoming trip. I asked her what her question was. She replied, "How can you go to Africa to help others, when there are so many unfortunate and homeless people here in America, in fact, right here in our community?" This opened the door for a ministering moment. I love ministering and teaching moments.

I replied to her first with a question of my own, "Have you ever been to Africa?" She replied in the negative. I used as an example a recent storm that rippled through several of North Carolina's one hundred counties, crippling many of the residents, destroying, in some cases, everything. I reminded her of the devastation. I brought back to her remembrance how many were without power for several days, as well as being without water for a few days. I emphasized to her how terrible it was for those families. She eagerly, and with excitement, agreed with my statement. With the same level of eagerness and excitement, I informed her that I had been to Africa before, more than once.

I brought the seril truth to her, that the families in North Carolina may have suffered these things for a few days, but the fact of the matter is, the families in most of Africa suffer theses very things on a daily basis. She looked in awe when I began to talk about little orphan children who slept on bare pavement, with straw walls and no electricity. I went on to speak of families sending their children to a well to prime the pump just to taste fresh water. I was feeling fairly good by now. I went on to explain how entire cities used generator power from seven at night to seven in the morning—those who were fortunate enough to own a portable generator.

I brought my compassionate point home by letting her know, in Africa, people lived like that every day of their lives. The coworker who told me the woman wanted to ask me a question, stood in the distance behind her, nodding her head in agreement, as if to say, "You really told her."

After laying out my compassionate facts, I closed by saying, "People in the United States may suffer tragedies; however, there are resources beyond imagination for them." I exclaimed, "Even the homeless in the United States have it made, compared to those in what we call 'third-world countries,' or underdeveloped countries. I made my case, and said, "Ma'am, that's how I can go to a foreign county when we have needy people in America."

MERCY

"Then he touched their eyes and said, "According to your faith, let it be done to you" (Matthew 9:29 KJV).

While on a missions trip to South Africa, we were instructed to carry on our possession several one-dollar bills. This was what we were to use when tipping the locals when we were out for dinner, or to tip the hotel staff, or the person shuttling us throughout the country. While out in the village of a particular town, we encountered a few native gentleman outside working. It seemed to me they were working extremely hard. I was moved by what seemed like a work ethic lacking from many in our country, America. I was compelled to give each of them one US dollar. Little did I know, there were several other villagers watching from a distance. When they had seen me give the one dollar to the gentlemen, it seemed like the entire village began running out, and gathered around me. Having a deep sense of mercy and compassion for them, I began to hand out one-dollar bills to all who crowded around me with their outstretched hands. There was one man who arrested my attention as I handed him the one-dollar bill. This man placed the one-dollar bill upon his forehead and began to shout, "Thank you, Jesus! Thank you, Jesus." My heart fluttered with both sympathy and empathy. These people did not appear to need a physical healing from blindness, yet I was reminded of the mercy Jesus showed towards those who were in need.

Merriam-Webster defines "mercy" in many ways. A couple that stands out when it comes to the Ministry of Missions are:

- a blessing that is an act of divine favor or compassion—*May God have mercy on us;*
- compassionate treatment of those in distress—*works of mercy among the poor*

One of the most popular verses among both Jews and Christians promoting social justice is Micah 6:8. It reads, "He has showed you, O man, what is good. And what does the Lord require of you? To act justly, and to love mercy, and to walk humbly with your God."

There are many who desire to know more about what this inspiring verse teaches on the issues of mercy.

The Ministry of Missions requires mercy. "Love mercy" contains the Hebrew word *hesed*, which means "loyal love," or "loving kindness." Along with justice, Israel was to provide mercy. Both justice and mercy are foundational to God's character (Psalm 89:14). God expected His people to show love to their fellow man, and to be loyal in their love toward Him, just as He was loyal to them (Micah 2:8-9; 3:10-11; 6:12).

Whenever one considers involving themselves in foreign missions, they must first search within themselves. Are you a person who understands and lives by what God requires of us? "He hath shewed thee, O man, what is good; and what doth the Lord require of thee, but to do justly, and to love mercy, and to walk humbly with thy God?" (Micah 6:8 KJV). The motivation for missions must be compassion and mercy.

MISSIONS: SEE THE NEED, AND FIND THE WAY

MEET THE NEEDS OF OTHERS

Missions see the need, then find a way to meet the need.

The Samaritan, who by all accounts is the sworn enemy of the Jews, goes out of his way to help someone who does not look like him, or belong to the same social or religious organizations. It was the custom of the Jews to love and help only those of their race. The Samaritan woman in John 4:9 says to Jesus, "The Jews have no dealings with the Samaritans." Jesus lived to serve others. As president and founder of Mark Rowden Ministry International, Inc., the focus for the ministry is to not only see needs, but to act to help those in need by our deeds and actions. Reverend Jacob Nomdae, a Lott Carey National Foreign Missions mission leader, once said, "If people can't find hope, hope must find them." Those words really resonated inside of me.

Pastor Noah Jasay, the pastor of one of our affiliate churches in Liberia, West Africa, who is a friend in ministry with whom I have built a strong ministry relationship, is very involved in missions to help others across the community and the country of his native land. Pastor Jasay and his wife Laisy are committed to missions. He accepted the mandate to train local pastors in the county, as well as to plant and reactivate churches in and outside of Sinoe County. His passion for missions and understanding that Missions is Ministry, led to him reactivating the only Baptist school in the county. Being likeminded about missions led to the beginning of the MRM missions in Liberia, West Africa.

While in conversation with him, he shared with me some of the needs in their country, as well as some of the local needs in their community. The pastor first mentioned the dire need for the roof to be fixed on one of the local schools that had been damaged by a storm during monsoon season. I asked to see some photos of the damaged roof, and I inquired as to what the cost of repairs would be. Once I received all of the requested information, I knew then in my heart that MRM could not see this need and not *find a way to meet the need*. Seeing and meeting needs is a process, one that involves relationship-building and establishing trust. I want to be very clear, with all missions in action, it is critical to build trust, a trust that gives the assurance that resources given to missions is in fact being used for its intended purposes.

MRM raised funds specifically for the replacement of the damaged roof. However, there was another need that was handled somewhat differently. At the same school, there was a need for computers. There were high school students who did not have enough computer skills to turn one on and off. The request was for two computers. My military background is in telecommunications and information technology (IT), and as a certified IT project manager, I understood clearly the importance and need for the use of technology. Instead of sending the requested two computers, we purchased a total of ten computers with the help of some mission-minded believers who contributed to this cause, which led to the development of a computer lab.

The computer lab would not only provide training for the students, but would also allow for citizens in the local community to utilize the computer lab for personal training and use as well. Some of the computers were previously shipped along with other supplies, while the remainder of the computers were carried over during one of our mission trips to Liberia. On a return missions trip to Liberia, one of the MRM ambassadors and I were taken to the school for a tour and update on the computer lab. Seeing the results of having more computers, and seeing the excitement on the faces of all of the children, inspired me tremendously; so much so, that MRM committed on the spot (not knowing how, but walking by faith) to provide twenty additional desktop computers. Within six months of our return to the United States, with most of the MRM funds being raised going towards renovations for the new MRM headquarters building, we were able to raise enough additional funds to ship six of the twenty computers. God is a wonderful provider, who has proven over and over again that He is still able to do exceedingly, abundantly above all we can ask or think.

COMPELLED TO ACT

Seeing a need and acting on it are two different things. The parable of the Good Samaritan is the story told by Jesus in the gospel of Luke 10:25-37, in which a

Samaritan man travelling a road stopped and helped a Jewish man who had been beaten, robbed, and left for dead.

The Samaritan people were viewed with contempt by Jewish people, and yet the Good Samaritan stopped to help the injured man. Jesus told the story to illustrate that a true neighbor helps her fellow human. In the New Testament book of Luke, this passage reveals a conversation between Jesus and a man who asked Jesus what the greatest command was. Jesus responded that the greatest commandment was to love God, and that the second greatest commandment was to love your neighbor. The man asked who his neighbor was, and Jesus responded by telling the story of the Good Samaritan. In the story, two Jewish men—both prominent religious leaders—had separately passed by the Jewish victim of the crime, but neither had stopped to help. When the Samaritan man came along, he stopped to help the injured man, put the man on his own donkey, took him to an inn, and paid the innkeeper to let the man stay and to take care of him.

True missions require this kind of actions. MRM was challenged in this area of ministry to being compelled to act similarly. Grace Baptist Church, under the leadership of Pastor Noah Jasay, was compelled to aid widows, senior citizens, and the blind with food, personal hygiene, and other personal necessities, when they themselves were in need. So, how is it that one needy group can help another needy group with tangible necessities? This is when those led by God see the need, and find the way to meet the need.

When there are needs on the mission field that require sending funds to the mission station, it is vitally important to establish a trust relationship with someone physically residing in the mission station area. Funds were sent directly to the point of contact, who in turn, ensured the local church helping provide the needs for the widows, senior citizens, and the blind were able, to purchase the needed items.

The Samaritan of Luke's narrative had a compassionate heart, a helping hand, and an unlimited concern. He gave up personal comfort, physical energy, and valuable time. (This is called *sacrifice*). I want to convey a strong message to the reader that missions ought to cost us something. Missions requires a commitment to humanity. The robbers beat him up; the priest and the Levite passed him up; and the Samaritan picked him up. The thief said,

"What's yours, is mine. I'll take it." The priest and Levite reasoned, "What's mine, is mine; I'll keep it." But the Samaritan said, "What's mine, is yours; we'll share it."

DOESN'T SEEK COMPENSATION

The Ministry of Missions does not seek compensation for services rendered. Matthew 10:8 teaches "Freely ye have received, freely give," which refers both to the working of miracles, and preaching of the Gospel. As they had these miraculous gifts freely imparted to them by Christ, they had them not of themselves, nor did they procure them at any charge, or expense of theirs, or purchase them with their money. We are to freely make use of our gifts and resources for the relief of the distressed, without insisting upon, or receiving any thing for the same.

This is not to say we should not accept any sort of compensation, for the Bible is clear: "The workman is worthy of his hire" (1 Timothy 5:18). However, the point is not to do ministry, especially mission work, expecting compensation.

When I was first asked by one of the pastors in Liberia, West Africa, to come to Africa and minister to their convention of twenty-seven churches, and to do some missionary work, as the founder and president of Mark Rowden Ministry International, Inc., my initial thought, to be honest, was, *How much are you going to pay me to come to Africa?* In my mind, I considered the travel expenses, lodging, meals, and the cost of just traveling to a foreign country. But thanks be unto God, my spirit reminded me that the Ministry of Missions will cost you something. I have lived by the saying "If God takes you to it, He will bring you through it."

I began to seek God through prayer, and discussions with other likeminded believers and MRM ambassadors. I concluded that if God truly was going to get the glory out of this, I had to depend on him to make provisions, and not rely on the very people who were in need of being ministered to for compensation for the mission trip.

Needless to say, through much prayer and generous contributions, I was able to make the mission trip. The people of Liberia were blessed through preaching, teaching, and outreach.

When we see the need, if we are sincere about spreading the gospel of Jesus Christ, we will find a way.

CHALLENGES OF MISSIONS

If we examine the scriptures carefully—especially Jesus's message—we will notice that the Gospel is full of challenges. "Come, follow me and I will make you fishers of men" (and women) is a challenge that requires full use of our abilities and resources (Matthew 4:19 KJV). When I made the commitment to live out the Great Commission, I had no idea of the challenges that came with it.

Have you ever traveled to a location either for business or pleasure? If you happen to experience car trouble while driving, that's frustrating, at the least. If you travel by air, and your flight is delayed due to weather conditions, or if you get bumped from the flight because it's overbooked, that's also frustrating. It will literally take you back to your BC days—you know, Before Christ, or Before Church—at least in my personal experience it did.

There is a difference, I believe, in being delayed when leaving for a trip than being delayed when returning from a trip, depending on if it is business or pleasure. I can remember one year, my wife Beverly and I went home to Houston, Texas, to visit family for the Christmas holidays. We drove from Fayetteville,

North Carolina, as we had done for several years. This particular year was a bad wintery year.

The drive to Houston was a fairly good one; no problems, and traffic was as expected for a holiday season. I felt pretty good after the seventeen-hour drive straight through. We enjoyed spending time with family, and they seemed to have enjoyed our being there. As our time on vacation came to an end, it was now time to get back on the road and head to North Carolina.

Beverly had to be back to her job at the Womack Army Hospital on Fort Bragg, and I had to be back for military formation at my unit on Fort Bragg. The weather report forecasted snow and ice throughout the states we had to travel through. If you have ever traveled from the East Coast to the West Coast, you know there are several states to travel across. The travel from Fayetteville, North Carolina, to Houston, Texas, has a dredged distance of nearly twelve hundred miles, through seven states, Texas being the longest of them all.

We were on Interstate 10, less than an hour and a half before the challenges began. Because of ice on the interstate, the highway patrol had the interstate blocked, and was detouring all traffic to another farm road. This detour had taken us about two hours off of the normal route.

If that was not bad enough, by the time we traveled through the state of Louisiana, and midway through Mississippi, the snow began to fall heavily. Our driving speed had now gone from approximately sixty miles per hour to about fifty miles per hour. This in itself would add a couple additional hours to the drive back. I am still talking about personal challenges that are frustrating. After a slow drive through snow fall, we finally made it through Alabama and Georgia, and were now headed into South Carolina. I could just feel North Carolina nearing, smiling as we passed through North Augusta, and nodding my head up and down with gladness as we traveled through Columbia, South Carolina.

As the snow continued to fall, and the roads were still icy, we approached I-95, and yes, I was saying in my mind, *It has be nearly twenty hours, but we are in the final stretch*. But as the old saying goes, when it rain, it pours. We were on I-95 for less than thirty minutes, when all of a sudden, the rear tire blew out.

Talk about being crushed in spirit. I found myself asking God, "What have I done to deserve this? Now we are broke down on the side of the road in the snow, and in the middle of the wee hour of the morning. What now?" I called for towing assistance, and they informed me due to the road conditions, it could be as long as a two-hour wait. No way did I desire in the least, having to wait two hours for help. I decided to pull the spare tire out and fix the flat myself. It was the most chilling experience of changing a flat tire ever. After about thirty minutes, the spare tire was on, and we were back on the road. Two hours later, Beverly and I were pulling into our driveway at our home. Did this challenging experience alter how I feel about going home to be with family? No. Would I do it all over again, considering how important I view spending time with family? Yes.

In comparison, I have an even stronger feeling about fulfilling the Great Commission. On one of the MRM International, Inc. mission trips to Liberia, West Africa, I was accompanied by a team of five ambassadors. I followed all of the steps that I will discuss in the chapter on Preparing for Mission Trips.

The trip was initially planned for the month of December. However, after several discussions with Pastor Noah Jasay—who was now an MRM ambassador in Liberia, and the pastor of Grace Baptist

Church—the decision was made to schedule an earlier mission trip for May. A team of interested and willing partners, along with ambassadors, was finalized within a couple of months.

The travel agency was contacted early on, and offered a very decent fare for travel to Monrovia in Liberia, West Africa. However, not all of the team was prepared to pay the cost for the travel. After talking back and forth with the travel agent, I was informed that the airfare that was quoted would no longer be available after three days. I informed the team of the increase in cost if we did not purchase the tickets within three days. Only three of the six team members were able to comply, myself included. Being concerned that if the team did not all purchase tickets at the same time—it could allow for travel difficulties—I asked the travel agent if they would allow us a few more days.

The favor of God prevailed. They extended us three additional days. After the additional three days had passed, three of the team members still were not ready to secure the travel expense. By now, in my mind I was thinking, *Maybe it is only meant for three of us to go.* Trying to stay focused, with an ear for the voice of God, I continued to talk with the travel agent, and by now, the cost had slightly gone up. I made the very hesitant decision to at least book the flight for three of the six who were scheduled to go. How bad could the end results be?

After paying the required fee, the agency booked three of us. I learned my first valuable lesson when scheduling a mission trip for a team of people. Now it was time for another conference call with the team, knowing that some resided in a different state. During the conference call, I went back over the list of logistical items from a previous conference call, only to find out some of the team did not have their passports. Talk about challenges. I later discovered that four of the six team members had not received their passports; two had applied, while the other two had an expired passport. After getting through that nail-biting period, now knowing that everyone had their passports and visa, you're probably wondering, whatever happened about getting everyone booked on the flight for the mission trip? That particular challenge was not yet over, but as previously mentioned, the cost was continually increasing.

Finally, one of the three remaining team members secured a seat on the same flight with me and two other team members. A week or so later, the remaining two members secured theirs also.

Wow, what a challenge. Now it was time for another conference call to discuss what would take place once in country as far as the teaching and preaching part of the mission, the crusade, and a site visit to one of the schools the ministry supports. Everyone was excited, all packed with travel snacks and more. The day was approaching for everyone to meet at John F. Kennedy Airport in New York. Monday could not come soon enough; that was the day we were scheduled to depart.

It was Thursday morning now. I received an email message from the travel agency informing me that the airline for our connecting flight in Brussels had been canceled due to a pilot strike. OMG! I thank God I was at a church attending a local citywide Blessing of the Badges ceremony. Had I been anywhere else, I believe I would have lost my mind. At that moment, I experienced every human emotion possible. I was numb. I got up and excused myself from the sanctuary. I went outside to contact the travel agent, who informed me that I had to contact the airline directly, and the only thing they could do was reimburse us for the flight because we'd purchased insurance coverage for the tickets.

I immediately called the airline, who very calmly apologized for the inconvenience, and informed me that the pilots were going on strike on the day we were scheduled to arrive. The airline agent politely offered me a later flight, which so happened to be one day before our scheduled return date. "When it rains, it pours" came alive in my life. I explained to the airline agent the date offered would not work for us, that we were missionaries, and it was a group of us traveling. She again apologized, and said there was nothing else that could be done. I did what I knew worked, for there is a portion of a passage in the Bible that says "The effectual fervent prayers of the righteous avail much" (James 5:16 KJV).

As I stood on the outside of the sanctuary nearly frantic, I asked every clergy member who passed me on their way inside for the ceremony to go into prayer with me, and I briefly explained why. I have always believed, and have taught, to be specific in our prayers. I spent the entire time of the Blessing of the Badge ceremony on the phone, calling every agency I thought could help, but to no avail. Hope began to dwindle. Because so much planning had taken place not only on our part, as the team traveling for the mission trip, but just as much planning on the part of the ministry team in Africa, I had no choice but to contact the point of contact in Liberia to sadly inform them that we would not be able to come.

I apologetically explained what had happened, and asked if we could reschedule our trip for another time. I could hear disappointment in his voice. I asked him what I could do to let the people know what happened, and to express my sincere regret. He said if I wanted, I could go live on African radio to express to the people of that region our deepest regrets. Now I had to contact the team to inform them. It seemed like double jeopardy. *Why, Lord, must I tell this depressing story all over again to a team of missionaries who I've been pressuring to get their shots, get their passports, get their visas, and be sure to pack completely at least one week in advance?* I had to inform a team of excited missionaries, who had done all that was required to make the trip.

But a still voice spoke to me, saying, "Lo, I am with you, always, even unto the end." Those words were not as comforting as I hoped. This day was one of the most challenging days of my life as a leader of people. I mustered up enough courage to call each individual, having to relive the pain of telling that wretched story over and over again. Thank God there were two married couples on the team, and that spared me of only having to tell the bad news only three more times. As I pondered the canceled flight departing from JFK, it dawned on me that we all had separate flights to JFK; meaning, we would have to cancel those flights and stand losing money spent for those flights. Just when I thought things couldn't get any worse.

I found myself questioning my decision to arrange the mission trip in the first place, but more than that, I found myself questioning God. I received a text message from our lead minister in Sinoe County, Liberia, encouraging me that they were all praying and trusting God. I could not wait until this day would end. Like a nightmare, I asked myself, *When will all of this end? Am I dreaming? If so, Lord, please wake me from this terror.*

As the day began to come to a close, I received an email from the airline stating they were able to find another airline that would serve as our connecting flight from Brussels. Praise the Lord. However, because the flights were purchased separately, the last three of the team to purchase their tickets would have to fly on a different flight than the three of us who'd purchased tickets at the same time. I notified the team, and informed them of the good news, along with the bad news. I told them if they were still interested in going, we would move forward. I offered time for them to talk it over amongst themselves, keeping in mind I had to let the airline know our decision as soon as possible. After some discussion, all agreed to move forward with the mission trip, even with the separate flights, realizing we all would arrive at the same time, reunite in Ghana, and fly together from Ghana to Monrovia. So now we were back on track, everyone, once again, excited.

Can I remind you that when we are doing the work as missionaries, the spiritual battle never really ends. The storms only become calm until the force of wind.

On Monday morning, I met one of the team members who resident in Fayetteville, North Carolina, in the same city as me. We arrived to Fayetteville Regional Airport for check-in, only for the attendant to inform us there was no flight for us. I reassured her there was a confirmed reservation, and we gave her the flight information. The attendant was able to find the flight in the system, but informed us that the flight had been canceled by someone. I asked why. She indicated that it was based on an email request to the airline regarding the procedure to cancel a fight if a connecting flight was canceled.

With an uneasy feeling, I let the attendant know that I'd made the request via email, but never indicated I wanted to cancel the flight. My mind went back to the day the airline contacted me to inform me of another flight, which had reopened the door for our mission trip. I said to God, "God, you didn't open this door to have it close in my face." I began to pray in my spirit, thanking God for reopening the door, and I rebuked everything that would come to steal my joy and attempt to void my blessing. Demonstrating such professionalism, the attendant said it was no problem; she would rebook us.

This process took longer than I expected, but nonetheless, we were now booked. We checked our bags, and off we went to security check-in. The line at the security checkpoint was extremely long; in fact, in the more than twenty years of flying from this airport, I had never seen the line as long as it was. No problem. All that was on my mind was that God had fixed it, and we are about to head to JFK. Once inside the terminal area, we walked to our boarding gate, only to discover the aircraft was backing out from the terminal. In my mind, this had to be a mistake; they'd changed the boarding gate.

There were people boarding at another gate, so I asked the attendant if it was the flight going to JFK. The attendant said no, and that we'd just missed boarding for that flight. Talk about the challenges of missions. I asked when the next flight to JFK was, because we had a flight to catch that afternoon to Africa. The attendant said she would put us on a standby flight. The word "standby" alone was discouraging. With a smile on her face, the attendant encouraged us, and told us that our chances to get on the standby flight were very high. Sure enough, as boarding began, our names came across the intercom system for boarding. The highest praise fell from my lips. Hallelujah!

As we sat on the plane waiting to pushback and taxi down the runway, an announcement came over the planes intercom stating the flight was delayed due to some mechanical issues. The pilot assured us the flight would depart as soon as possible. My concern was even though the overseas flight from JFK was not leaving until later, we had already missed the original flight, and now the flight we were aboard was delayed. An hour passed, and we were still sitting on the runway outside the terminal gate. I was growing concerned, because now time was against us. By the time the flight finally was ready for takeoff, it was mathematically impossible we would make it to JFK in time for our flight.

I contacted the rest of the team members who'd departed from Atlanta and were already at JFK. The Team member in Atlanta who was booked on the flight with me, I inquired to see if the airline would let him book a seat on the flight with the other three team members, one of whom was his wife. I could not help but think of what I often say to congregants from the pulpit; that in my darkest moments, I get excited, because I know it is then when God will step in and deliver me out of my darkest moments. I could see spiritual darkness looming once again. The challenges of missions.

As soon as we landed in New York, I immediately began calling the airline to ask about the possibility of getting on the flight to Africa. I was told it was not possible, but was assured with no problems that we could get booked on a flight the next day. Afterwards, I reached out to find out whether or not the other team member was able to get booked on the flight with the other members. He said they were putting him on standby. I said to him, "Do not let them put you on standby. Just wait until the following day, so that the three of us can fly together." I knew he really wanted to have the chance to fly with his wife; however, standby was not our best option for an overseas flight. We got a room at a nearby hotel I frequented when traveling from JFK.

His wife and two others on the team had to travel without us. Keep in mind, I was the only one on the team who had traveled to Africa previously, except for the ambassadors from North Carolina who'd served in the United States Special Forces, and had been on military missions to Africa years ago. My concern was for the ones who had never been out of country prior to this missions trip. Well, our troubles did not stop there.

The next day, after we'd gotten to JFK airport from our hotel, when we arrived at check-in, we were told that one of the names was not on the reservation. I have always heard that God has a sense of humor, but this just wasn't funny at all. It appeared that when the one team member who'd asked to go on standby initially, the airline had removed him from our flight; and once he'd told them he did not want to be on standby, apparently he was never added back to the original manifest. I am sharing this one challenging event not to scare you from missions rather to encourage you, knowing "the just shall live by faith". All still was not lost. Once again we went into prayer believing this all was happening to strengthen our faith and to draw us nearer to the God we profess we trust in. After much pleading with the airline and sharing our eventful journey and we hadn't even made it out of the United States, they were able to get all of us on the scheduled flight from JFK to Monrovia. We ended up flying with a connecting flight on one of the African jetliners that would now take us to Ghana. Off we go, great flight across the friendly skies. We arrived in Ghana and proceeded to check in for our connecting flight to Monrovia. And yes you guessed it, to good to be true. Now we were told that the other Ambassador who was with me in North Carolina was not on the manifest to Monrovia. I could do nothing but laugh out loud and say to him "Now you really didn't think the devil was going to pick on everyone but you now did you?" It was now his turn to be picked out to be picked on. We presented documents showing he was on the reservation with us. After several minutes passed the airline person returned and confirmed he was in fact on the reservation. You are probably wondering where the other three team members are now. Well, because we had to stay overnight in New York, their Ghana flight had already departed to Monrovia. No problem, I made arrangements for them to stay with a family I resided with on a previous mission trip. Unfortunately, we had chartered an aircraft that could not be rescheduled with such short notice, therefore the other three team members had to take the flight on to Monrovia. So what do the three of us do once we arrive to Monrovia? I knew you would guess it correct, pray for another miracle. Once we arrived to Monrovia the in country Ambassador had rented a vehicle to drive us to Sinoe County. Sinoe County is normally about a five hour drive over rough terrain. We waited and waited at the airport but there was no one there to pick us up. When I made contact with our point of contact he said the rental vehicle had broken down on the way to pick us up.

We waited at a restaurant near the airport for about two hours until another vehicle was accommodated. Night began to fall, and the vehicle had now arrived, but there was not enough fuel in the vehicle to get us to our destination. We drove around town looking for fuel. We finally found a place to get fuel, but there was also the challenge of having to deal with price gougers.

But finally we were on the road to our destination. The weather turned really bad, and the rain began to fall as if it was monsoon season. The already rough terrain of the roads were saturated with rain, which made them near impossible to pass. What was supposed to be a five-hour drive became a twelve-hour drive, with three of us cramped in the back seat of a mini SUV with luggage.

We finally arrived to Sinoe County at the break of morning the next day. As we were exiting the vehicle at the mission hotel, as ambassador William Hill from Fayetteville, North Carolina, exited the vehicle, the driver slammed his door closed, not realizing the ambassador's fingers were in the door. He didn't understand that we were saying his fingers were in the door. I rushed to open the door, only to realize his finger was broken. (When it rains, it pours). The challenges of missions. Nonetheless, we made it through it all, and accomplished the mission we set out to do. To God be the glory.

In order for the ministry of missions to be effective, one must endure the challenges of missions, and have a compassionate heart, helping hand, and unlimited concern for the needy. The term "compassion" has its linguistic roots in the Latin words *com* (with) and *pati* (suffering). When Jesus saw the blind men, for example, he "had compassion on them, and touched their eyes. Immediately they received their sight and followed him" (Matthew 20:34 KJV).

When he saw groups yearning for his teaching, "he had compassion on them, and healed their sick" (Matthew 14:14 KJV). Christ noted the confusion of the people in the crowd following him, and "had compassion on them, because they were like sheep without a shepherd" (Mark 6:34 KJV).

All these examples of Christ's compassion have two things in common: First, Jesus *notices* the people around him. This tells us that compassion is only possible when we are attuned to others. If we're absorbed in our own feelings, problems, worries, and desires, we will overlook the needs of those God puts in our path, and ignore the opportunity to help them. Second, Jesus *responds* to people, instead of reacting to them. He listens to the ten lepers, rather than being irritated that they're interrupting his conversation (Luke 17:12-19 KJV). He takes time to speak with the woman who touches the hem of his garment, instead of simply chastising her for lacking appropriate boundaries (Matthew 9:20 KJV).

Throughout Jesus's ministry, he constantly focused on developing relationships with all kinds of persons, and then demonstrated his love for them. The Great Commission calls us to join him in this ministry. In the context of relationships and day-to-day activity, we are invited to participate selflessly as ambassadors for Christ. To do this we must have a compassionate heart, be willing to get into the trenches of the ministry call to missions, and have a genuine concern for the needy.

In having a compassionate heart, one must be willing to give up personal comfort, time, and energy. Missions are not a vacation. It requires commitment and sacrifice. Missions see the need, then finds a way to meet the need. Remember the story of the Samaritan mentioned earlier? The Samaritan of this narrative had a compassionate heart, a helping hand, and unlimited concern. He gave up personal comfort, physical energy, and valuable time. Missions ought to cost us something. Missions require a commitment to humanity.

PREPARATION FOR MISSIONS

Preparation for missions is a major undertaking. Having a detailed check list will help the planning of your foreign missions trip, and make it so much easier. Shots and other medical requirements will differ from country to country. The following is an example and a guide for Liberia, West Africa.

VACCINES AND MEDICINES

Make sure you are up-to-date on routine vaccines before every trip. These vaccines include the measles-mumps-rubella (MMR) vaccine; diphtheria-tetanus-pertussis vaccine; varicella (chickenpox) vaccine; polio vaccine; and your yearly flu shot. Ask your physician to prescribe for you diarrhea pills for travelers, as well as malaria pills.

Health recommendation: Yellow fever is a risk in Liberia, so CDC recommends this vaccine for all travelers who are nine months of age or older.

Country entry requirement: The government of Liberia *requires* proof of yellow fever vaccination for all travelers, except infants.

Hepatitis A	CDC recommends this vaccine because you can get hepatitis A through contaminated food or water in Liberia, regardless of where you are eating or staying.
Malaria	You will need to take prescription medicine before, during, and after your trip to prevent malaria. Your doctor can help you decide which medicine is right for you, and also talk to you about other steps you can take to prevent malaria. See more detailed information about malaria in Liberia.
Typhoid	You can get typhoid through contaminated food or water in Liberia. CDC recommends this vaccine for most travelers, especially if you are staying with friends or relatives, visiting smaller cities or rural areas, or if you are an adventurous eater.

Rabies	Rabies can be found in dogs, bats, and other mammals in Liberia, so CDC recommends this vaccine for the following groups: • Travelers involved in outdoor and other activities (such as camping, hiking, biking, adventure travel, and caving) that put them at risk for animal bites. • People who will be working with or around animals (such as veterinarians, wildlife professionals, and researchers). • Children, because they tend to play with animals, might not report bites, and are more likely to have animal bites on their head and neck.

FLIGHTS

The best departure location for flights to Africa from the United States, in my personal experience, is a departure from JFK Airport in New York. However, there are flights from Atlanta Hartsfield as well.

Some considerations: If flying from JFK, and the flight to Africa is scheduled for departure at eight o'clock in the morning, careful planning must be done for flights from your point of embarkation, i.e. schedule a flight from Fayetteville, North Carolina, or your departure home city in order to get to JFK at least four hours before departure time.

With this in mind, it is recommended the traveler arrives to the departing airport the day before if it is not in the city from which you are departing, and get a hotel room. There are airport hotels that are not too expensive, and they have shuttles to and from the airport.

Coordination must be made for transportation upon arrival to Monrovia, Liberia, to the hotel, or to your mission destination. Coordination must be made for the hotel for the number of days of stay in your mission city. The number of days depends on the day of arrival. In-country flights to the more rural areas, such as Greenville, Liberia, (Sinoe County) only fly on Mondays, Wednesdays, and Fridays, once a day. This is not an issue for most of the more suburban cities. Hotel accommodations then must be arranged for the number of days of stay for whatever location the mission trip will be conducted.

Return flight to Monrovia from the mission site location must be made (keeping in mind the previously mentioned days of air travel from the mission site back to Monrovia). Return travel arrangement must factor in departure time, and date from mission city, to JFK, or whichever return airport of your choice.

Two flights are available for most airlines, one in the morning and one in the afternoon.

PASSPORT/VISA

Individuals traveling to Liberia must have a valid **passport** and **visa**. You must allow forty-five to sixty days when applying for a passport. You can expedite passports for additional fees. For first time overseas travelers who may not know, a visa is separate from your passport. You will be required to present your shot records upon arrival to Liberia. You are required to fill out a customs form prior to going through customs. If you do not have the form filled out, they will make you get out of line, go get the form, then get back in what is *always* a very lengthy line.

Prior to traveling to Liberia, I recommend that all persons going read up on the history and customs of the country. Most travel agents will provide a handout in your packet (if a travel agent is used).

Speaking of travel agents. Most travel agents require a certain number of travelers before they will allow use of their service. (Every agency differs, however.) It is highly recommended to use a travel agent because they will do 90 percent of the leg work for you. Also, ticket cost is cheaper when using travel agents, and they will include flights and hotel cost to include baggage cost. (Passengers are allowed two checked baggage, regardless.)

People who are taking long mission trips should consider the following when they pack their carry-on bag: a small personal pillow, or one of the popular cushion neck rests; your medicines; something to snack on, not only for during the flight, but while waiting for connecting flights, which may require long layovers.

This is just a snapshot of some of the logistics to consider for travel to Liberia, West Africa, and will also assist in other foreign mission travels.

MAKING A GLOBAL DIFFERENCE THROUGH THE MINISTRY OF MISSIONS

The Ministry of Missions is a guide to effective mission preparation and execution, with real-world mission testimonies, as well as examples of how missionary partnerships can enhance global missions, and at the same time fulfill the Great Commission of teaching, evangelism, and salvation. Mark Rowden is a visionary pastor, theologian, evangelist, community leader, educator, retired veteran, and patriarch of his family. Birthed from his desire to fulfill the Great Commission, and to teach all nations, Mark Rowden Ministries International, Inc. (MRM) was founded in June 2016. Dr. Rowden and his wife Beverly enjoy ministering to God's people through the Word by teaching a practical application for Christian living.

Dr. Rowden serves the people of God in many roles, and offers himself to multiple community organizations and activities. It is the goal of MRM to educate, inspire, and empower the people of God through teaching, reaching, and restoring. This aspect of the ministry is accomplished through the World Outreach Worship Center (WOW). MRM, through its partners and committed affiliates, provides scholarships for deserving high school graduates enrolling in colleges around the globe. He has always had a heart for missions, and believes true missions are mission in action.

As he researched opportunities to support other mission organizations, he realized that often there was a lack of accountability, as well as limitations that individual organizations working alone could accomplish. He also learned that most organizations often present their own mission objectives, and do not allow or accept suggested projects. Dr. Rowden founded Mark Rowden Ministry International, Inc., creating a hub for individuals and organizations of any size to work together to meet the need of others. Mark Rowden Ministry International, Inc. works differently.

Our affiliate partners submit specific needs that they researched, or have been alerted to, within the United States, or worldwide, for consideration. Whether responding to a request for school supplies in North Carolina, replacing damaged roofs on school buildings in Liberia, West Africa, or providing personal hygiene items in Malawi, South Africa, collectively our affiliates and ambassadors complete projects, and reach goals that individuals and organizations working alone might not be able to accomplish.

BIBLIOGRAPHY

Barnes, Albert. "Commentary on Matthew 5:16." "Barnes' Notes on the New Testament." http://www.studylight.org/commentaries/bnb/matthew-5.html. 1870.

Gill, John. "Commentary on Matthew 5:16." "The New John Gill Exposition of the Entire Bible." http://www.studylight.org/commentaries/geb/matthew-5.html. 1999.